PINGU

Annual

£5.50

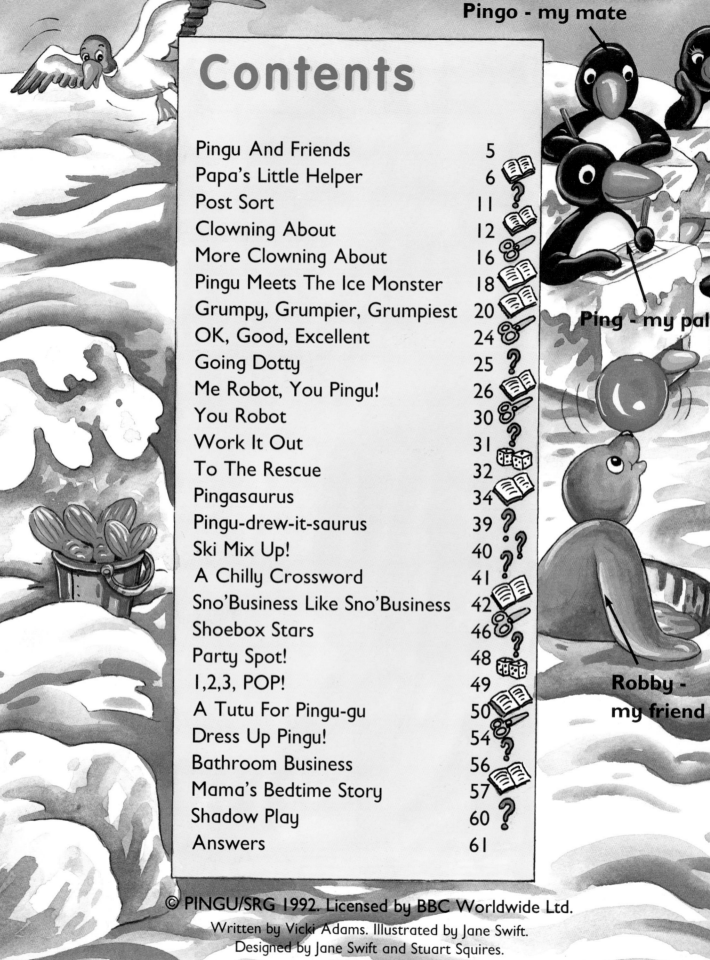

Contents

Pingo - my mate

Ping - my pal

Robby - my friend

Written by Vicki Adams. Illustrated by Jane Swift.
Designed by Jane Swift and Stuart Squires.
Published by
Grandreams Limited.
Jadwin House, 205/211 Kentish Town Road, London, NW5 2JU.
Printed in Belgium.

Pingu and Friends

Pingi - my girlfriend

Papa - my post-penguin dad

Professor Pengalo - my teacher

Grandma - Grandma!

Grandpa - Mama - Mama! Grandpa!

Pinga - my little sister

Pingu - me!

Papa's Little Helper

1. "Please, Papa!" Pingu pleaded. "I promise not to be naughty. Please, please, please, please let me help you on your post round.
Please! I'll be a great help. I'm a fast learner and, and..."
Papa looked at Pingu. "Remember what happened last time..."

2. "Was that the time I let those seagulls have a ride in the mail bag?" said Pingu. "I thought they'd be helpful. I didn't think they'd fly off with all the mail."

3. "Well, Pingu," said Papa. "If you promise to do as I say, then you can come. But if anything goes wrong this time, you won't be allowed to help again."

4. "Papa! Wake up!" said Pingu. "Today's the day - today I'm Papa's postie helper! I can't wait!" Papa opened one eye and looked at Pingu, "I'm awake."

5. "Now eat up Pingu," said Papa. "We must be on time." Pingu looked up at the clock and took a sip of juice. "I'm ready!" he slurped.

6. Papa picked up his bag of mail - it was a big bag full of lots of letters and parcels. "We're going to be very busy, Pingu," smiled Papa.

7. Papa sorted the letters out into bundles and Pingu poked them through the letterboxes. "We do make a good team," said Papa proudly, as he drove along.

8. "It's 10 o'clock," said Papa. "Do you know what that means, Pingu?"
"Break time!" yelled Pingu. "Yum, I'll drink my icy shake." Just as Pingu went to sip his drink - it flew out of his wing... and jumped into the mail bag. "Waak!" Pingu was caught by surprise. "OOOPS!"

9. "It's like a mail milkshake in there!" sighed Papa.
"Papa, I'm very sorry," said Pingu. "All the letters will be very tasty."
"Letters are not for eating!" Papa replied.

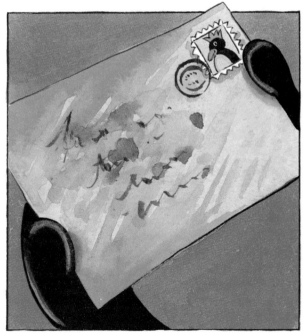

10. "What are we going to do?" cried Pingu. "We can't read the addresses anymore. Papa, I'm sorry, sorry..."
"Don't worry, it was an accident," Papa smiled. "Let's have a think..."

11. "How can we deliver our letters?" said Papa out loud.
"We could open them," said Pingu, "to see who they are to."
"No," said Papa. "We can't deliver opened letters."

12. "Let's ask Madame Penski to look into her crystal ball," cried Pingu. "She would be able to see who the letters are to!" Papa shook his head - Pingu tried to think of another way.

13. "Papa!" cried Pingu. "I've got a great idea! It's the best idea I've ever had!"
Papa looked at the little penguin, "I hope it's a very good idea, Pingu."

14. "We'll visit the rest of the igloos on the post round," started Pingu, "and ask each penguin if they have any friends who live in another country." "Go on," said Papa.

15. "We can find out where their friends live," Pingu continued. "And look at the stamps on the letters - there are only ten letters left in the mail bag and each one is from a different country!"

16. "That will take a long time," said Papa. "There are 30 igloos left on our round. But it is a very clever idea. Come on. The sooner we get started the sooner we can go home."

17. After a while, Pingu had delivered all the mail by looking at the stamps and asking questions. "I'm so pleased," yawned Pingu, "that today is nearly over."

18. "Pingu," said Papa. "You've been a great help - do you want to help me again tomorrow?"
"No thank you, Papa," smiled Pingu. "I don't think mail and Pingu mix!"

Post Sort

Waak! Pingu's done it again! Look at the stamps and see if you can match them to the country the letters were sent from. Read the names and addresses carefully to find the clues.

Turn to page 61 for the answers.

Mr Kangaroo
1 Bush Road
Australia

Miss Thistle
10 Tartan Way
Scotland

A.

B.

C.

D.

Mr and Mrs Dragon
2 Leek Place
Wales

Mr and Mrs Clogs
The Canal
Holland

Clowning about!

"PINGU!"

Pingu looked out the window to see Ping and Robby jumping up and down like yo-yos.

"Waak!" he yelled. "What's up?"

"Come on," his friends called.

"The circus is in town."

"Excellent!" said Pingu.

The three friends raced over to the circus.

"This is so-ooo exciting," sighed Ping.

"Look," said Pingu, "at the huge tent!"

"Look," cried Ping, "at the tiny horses!"

"Look!" yelled Robby.

"At what?" asked Pingu.

"I don't know," Robby replied. "Just, um, look!"

They watched as all the circus performers raced about getting ready for the big show.

"I'd love to join the circus," said Pingu.

"Me too!" agreed Ping.

"ME-EE TO-OO!" yelled Robby.

"Let's do it," said Pingu. "Come on, we'll have to find the Ring Master. He'll give us all a job."

The three friends raced about looking for the Ring Master.

They found him in the big tent wearing a sequinned jacket and shiny top hat.

"Are you the Ring Master?" asked Pingu.

The Ring Master nodded, "How can I help you?"

"We want to join the circus," the three friends replied.

"Well, do you now?" he smiled down at them. "Follow me."

Pingu, Ping and Robby followed the older penguin into the ring.

"Climb up there," the Ring Master pointed to the ladder leading up to the tightrope.

"Way up there?" shivered Robby. The three friends started to climb the ladder.

"It's too high!" wailed Ping.

"I feel giddy," whined Robby.

"I want to get down!" cried Pingu.

"Um," said the Ring Master. "I don't think you're cut out to be trapeze artists. "Can you ride a pony?"

"Looks, easy," said Pingu.

The three friends climbed up onto the small ponies but before the Ring Master had walked two steps, they had all tumbled to the ground.

"Ponies aren't for you, either," he smiled kindly.

"What about taming lions?" he asked.

"No! NO! NOOO!" they all cried at once.

"Juggling?" suggested the Ring Master, as he threw Pingu, Ping and Robby a set of juggling balls.

The three friends were eager to please the Ring Master. They started to juggle - it was no use, Pingu and his friends were not jugglers.

"Um, juggling is out too," the Ring Master took off his hat and rubbed his head. "What about... wait here." He left the three friends wondering what was happening. He returned carrying a pile of shoes, clothes and colourful wigs.

"Put on these," he said. "These will be your clown costumes."

14

"We're going to be clowns!" cried Pingu. "Great!"

Soon the three clowns were throwing buckets of water at each other, tripping over and falling about.

"Yes," said the Ring Master. "You'll make very good clowns. The big show begins at 8 tonight - please be on time."

Pingu and his friends set about practising and practising for their big performance.

It was not long before the little hand was on the 8 and the big hand was on the 12. Show time!

Pingu and his friends were the stars of the show - the audience clapped and cheered. And clapped and cheered.

"WAAK!" said Pingu, when the show was over. "That was hard work!"

"Ah," smiled the Ring Master, rubbing his hands together. "You were the stars of my show. How would you like to join my circus and tour the world."

Pingu looked at Robby, Robby looked at Ping, and Ping looked at Pingu.

"Thank you very much, Ring Master," said Pingu as he rubbed his flippers. "But we think being clowns is just hard work."

More Clowning About...

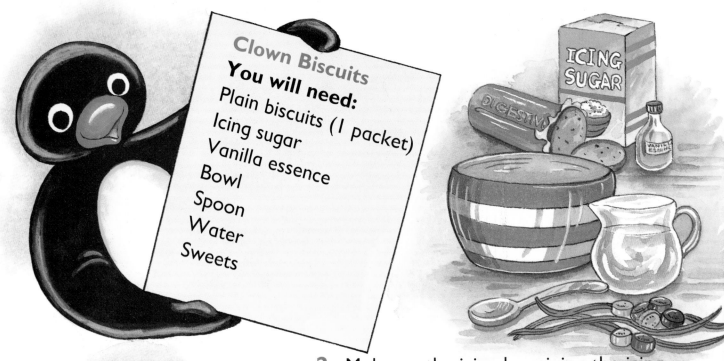

Clown Biscuits

You will need:
Plain biscuits (1 packet)
Icing sugar
Vanilla essence
Bowl
Spoon
Water
Sweets

2. Make up the icing by mixing the icing sugar and water together, then adding a few drops of vanilla essence into the mixture. Mix it well - if you think your icing is too thick, then add more water.

1. Before you start, wash your hands!

3. Spread the icing over each biscuit then make up a clown's face using your sweets. Liquorice is great for mouths and eyebrows, and wine gums are very good for eyes and noses.

Clown Mask
You will need:
Round paper plate
Piece of elastic (to attach your mask)
Shiny paper
Safe glue or sticky tape
Round-ended scissors
Coloured/shiny paper
Wool

1. Turn your paper plate over and start designing your clown face.
   You can paint all over it, then stick stars shapes on for eyes, a banana shape for the mouth, and a doughnut shape for the nose.

2. Stick the wool on to make a woolly wig or beard.

3. Make two holes for your eyes. Also make two holes, just as Pingu has done, to tie your piece of elastic - you need this to keep your mask on!

4. WAAK! You're finished - perhaps you could make another one for one of your friends.

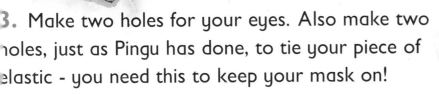

Pingu Meets the Ice Monster

1. _____

_____

2. _____

3. _____

_____

4. _____

_____

WAAK! What is happening in this story? Look at the pictures then tell the story in your own words. You can tell it out loud or write it in the spaces below the pictures. Will it have a happy ending?

5. _____

6. _____

_____

_____

7. _____

8. _____

_____

_____

Pingu and Ping were on their delivery round. They were delivering Cheer-You-Up-Quick icy blocks to all the sad penguins in their neighbourhood. There was only one more door left to be knocked on.

KNOCK! KNOCK!

"Go away!" growled the door.

"The door's growling at us!" cried Ping.

"It's not the door," said Pingu. "It's that grumpy old penguin."

"We're leaving an icy block for you, Mr Grumpy," called Pingu cheekily. "Come on, Ping, let's go home."

The two penguins did just that.

"He is the grumpiest of grumpy penguins," said Pingu. "I think we should play a trick on him. Not a mean trick," said Pingu. "I want to take the grump out of Mr Grumpy."

"He might be grumpy for a reason," said Ping.

The next day, Pingu waddled over to Mr Grumpy's igloo. He climbed onto a barrel, then looked through the dirty window.

"That's why Mr Grumpy's grumpy!" Pingu watched as Mr Grumpy creaked about the room in an old wheelchair.

"Poor, Mr Grumpy!" sighed Pingu. "He can't waddle!"

Pingu jumped down from the barrel, and ran to the front door.

KNOCK! KNOCK!

"Go, away!" growled Mr Grumpy.

"But..." Pingu started.

"LEAVE ME ALONE!"

Pingu made his way home sadly, "Waak, I wish I could help," he thought out loud.

Pingu found Mama in the garden and told her everything about Mr Grumpy.

"Ah," she said. "Perhaps we can help him." So Mama put on her thinking cap.

"He sounds like he's a very proud penguin," she said. "So we will have to help him but pretend we're not helping him. I've got an idea."

Mama disappeared into the garden shed. She tapped and hammered - she was making a racket!

"MAMA!" called Pingu. "What are you doing?"

"You'll have to wait and see," Mama yelled back.

Pingu wondered what Mama was up to. He was still wondering, when he woke up the next morning.

"Good morning," called Mama. "Time to get up. Today's the day we take the grump out of Mr Grumpy!" Mama led Pingu and Pinga into the front garden. "Tah dah!" Mama had made a snowmobile. It was a very special snowmobile, it could move outside as well as inside.

"Mama, you're a..." cried Pingu.

"Genius," Mama finished Pingu's sentence for him. "Come on. We're going visiting."

"I've made some frosties for him too," smiled Pinga.

"Let's go!" cried Pingu.

Soon they all arrived at Mr Grumpy's igloo.

"Look, Mr Grumpy!" cried Pingu happily.

"Go away!" growled Mr Grumpy.

"Don't be a silly penguin," said Mama sternly. "If you're going to act like a baby penguin then

we're going to treat you like a baby penguin."

"What do you want, then?" he replied.

"I want you to try out my new snowmobile," said Mama. "I would be very grateful. And Pinga would like you to try her biscuits. You don't have to if you don't want to. But it would be very kind of you."

Slowly Mr Grumpy's door creaked open. "I suppose I could. Come in."

"Now, Mr Grumpy," said Mama. "Down to business."

It was not long before Mr Grumpy was zooming about on the snowmobile and munching biscuits.

"I haven't been outside in years!" he smiled. "This is great..."

Pingu winked at Mama.

"Ah," Mr Grumpy grinned. "This was a trick! You're helping out an old, ungrateful penguin."

Mama nodded.

"I can't thank you enough," said Mr Grumpy. "But there is one thing you should know if we're going to be friends. My name's Mr Smiley - my friends call me Smiley."

OK, Good, EXCELLENT!

WAAK! Make up a chart, writing down all the jobs that you do on one side - then leave a space next to each one. Just like Pingu has done. When you have finished a job, write in how well you have done (OK, Good or Excellent) or draw in stars, the more stars the better you think you've done your job. Look, Pingu's filled out his chart already.

Pingu's Chart	MONDAY	TUESDAY	WEDNESDAY	THURSDAY	FRIDAY	SATURDAY	SUNDAY
FEEDING THE FISH	☆☆	EXCELLENT	GOOD	GOOD	OK		
HELPING PAPA	GOOD	OK	☆☆☆	OK	EXCELLENT		
MAKING MY BED	OK	OK	GOOD	☆☆	☆		
BRUSHING MY BEAK	EXCELLENT	GOOD	☆☆	OK	EXCELLENT		

My Chart	MONDAY	TUESDAY	WEDNESDAY	THURSDAY	FRIDAY	SATURDAY	SUNDAY
WASH THE DISHES							
DRY THE DISHES							
MAKING MY BED							
TIDYING MY ROOM							
PUT THE RUBBISH OUT							
PICK UP RUBBISH IN GARDEN							

Going Dotty!

Pingu's been drawing, but what is it? He's got to stop, he's seeing dots before his eyes. Can you finish Pingu's drawing for him by joining all the dots?

See page 61 for the answer.

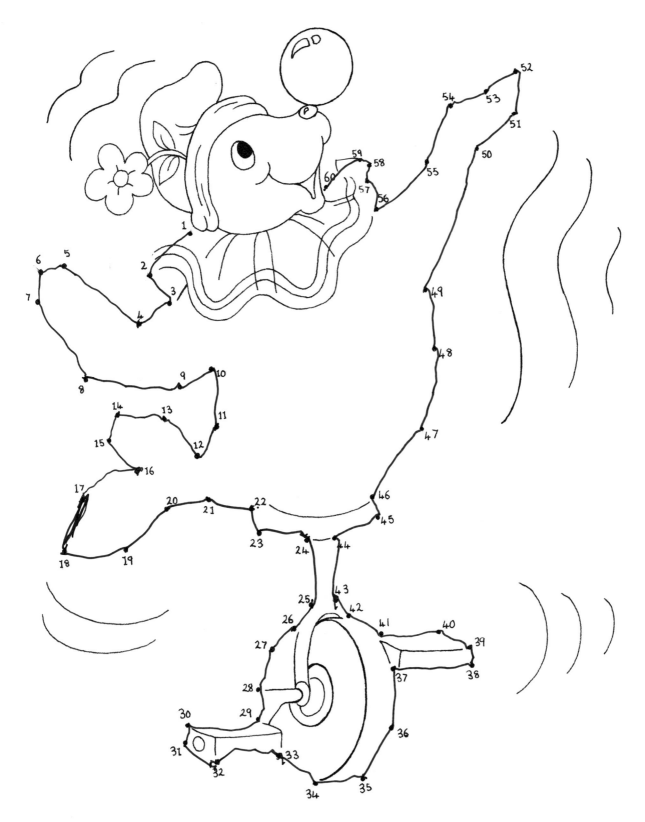

1. KNOCK! KNOCK! Pingu opened up one eye and pulled the blanket over his head. "It's sleep-in time!" he yawned and closed both his eyes.

CREAK! "Pingu, here's a parcel for you," whispered Mama, as she gently shook him to wake him up. Pingu sat up straight, "WAAK! It's arrived!" He started to rip the paper off his package.

2. "I've been waiting for you," cried Pingu. "Where have you been?" "Can-not an-swer ques-tion, need bat-ter-ies, need bat-ter-ies..." Pingu found them in the box and popped them into his back.

3. The robot clunked into action. "My name is Nut, your name is Pingu. Get out of bed and go to the toilet." Nut pushed him towards the bathroom. "But..."

4. When Pingu returned, Nut had cleaned the whole house and was cooking breakfast. Mama and Papa sat twiddling their wings. Nut wouldn't even let them read a book!

5. "Good morning," smiled Pingu. "Have you met Nut?" Mama and Papa nodded. "She will be great help around the house, doing odd jobs...". "She's doing all the jobs, Pingu," smiled Mama.

6. "Ah, this is the life," sighed Mama. "Why didn't we get a robot years ago?" "Where's my pipe?" yawned Papa. "Oh, thank you Nut!" Nut zoomed off to find another job to do.

7. It was not long before Nut was doing everything. He washed and cleaned, dusted and flustered, he rubbed and he scrubbed. Everything sparkled and shone.

8. "Nut won't even let us clean our beaks by ourselves!" sighed Pingu.
"You-do-not-clean-your-beak-as-well-as-I-do..." croaked Nut.
"I like cleaning my beak!" cried Pingu. "I'm a good beak cleaner!"

9. "I'm bored," sighed Pingu. "I'm bored, bored, bored, bored... WAAK!" Pingu stamped his flipper on the floor. Pinga looked up at him, "I'm bored too! I'm sick of just playing. I want to do something."

10. Pingu and Pinga made their way to school as usual. "We have to do something about that robot," said Pingu. "I'll ask Professor Pengalo if he can help - he knows everything."

11. When they arrived at school, Pingu nearly fell over his flippers trying to get to Professor Pengalo. Before the older penguin had a chance to say "Waak!", Pingu had told him all about Nut.

12. "Ah," said Professor. "We can't have that, now. Come along, Pingu. Introduce me to your little metal friend and I'll see what I can do." They found Nut cleaning the side of the igloo.

13. "That does it," said Professor Pengalo as he put Nut back together. "There's still one thing he will do." "What's that?" asked Pingu. "You'll just have to wait to find out," smiled Professor Pengalo.

14. The two little penguins went to bed early that night - they were tired out. But soon it was time to get up. RINGGGG! RINGGGG! Pingu opened one eye - "Excellent! You're an alarm robot."

You Robot!

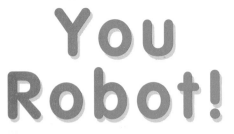

Have you ever wanted to be a robot? Well, Pingu's got some ideas for you. The most important thing to remember is... USE-YOUR-IM-AG-IN-A-TION.

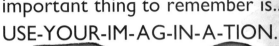

WAAK!

You will need:

**One big box (Body)
Small boxes
Cardboard tubes
Straws
Plastic
Sticky tape
Buttons
Ribbon
Shiny paper
Crayons, Paint, Felt tip pens
Anything you can think of - but make sure it's rubbish!**

Things to Remember

The big box is your body, so it has to be big enough for you to climb into.
Long cardboard tubes or rolled up cardboard make great arms and legs. Use lots of colour and flair.
Make sure that everything you stick onto your robot suit has a purpose.
You can join the arms and legs to the body by threading ribbon or string through holes.

Work it Out!

WAAK! Pingu's bored and wants to do a job to help Mama - but you know what Nut's like. Race through the maze to find out what Pingu can do to help - then help Nut to find out his job.

See answers on page 61.

To the Rescue!

33

Pingasaurus

"Mama, I want a dinosaur," yawned Pingu. "It's not possible, dinosaurs are extinct," Mama replied.

"What does that mean?" asked Pingu.

"It means that there are no dinosaurs left," Mama explained.

"I saw one today," said Pingu. "It was huge - it had big horns and a..."

Mama looked at Pingu, "No, Pingu, I know you didn't see a dinosaur today." "Good night, Pingu," said Mama.

Pingu fell asleep and dreamed about Woolly Mammoths and Tricerotops.

When Pingu woke up he went outside for a walk. "Mammoth footprints!" he cried when he spied big splotches in the snow. "I've found dinosaur footprints!" he yelled.

Mama and Papa rushed outside to look at the 'footprints', "Pingu, they're not dinosaur footprints, the rubbish barrels have been collected. They just look like footprints."

"Pingu," said Mama. "Dinosaurs are extinct. You won't find fresh dinosaur footprints."

Pingu continued on his way, he turned to go down a little path. Suddenly he bumped into something.

"Ouch!" Pingu rubbed his head. "I don't believe it!"

Pingu opened his eyes as wide as he could.

"A Woolly Mammoth!" he cried. "And not just footprints - a whole Woolly Mammoth!"

"Good morning," boomed the Mammoth. "How very nice to bump into somebody. My name is Fuzz and I was beginning to think..."

"You're a Woolly Mammoth, aren't you?" asked Pingu.

Fuzz looked down at himself. "Yes, I am woolly and I am very large," he said. "So I might as well be a woolly mammoth. Yes... that sounds about right."

"You're coming with me," said Pingu.

"Oh good," said Fuzz. "I hope you have more to offer than iced tea - I am quite fed up with iced tea."

"You can eat whatever you want!" cried Pingu.

Pingu and Fuzz ran nearly the whole way home.

"A proper meal!" cried Fuzz.

"A real Woolly Mammoth," cried Pingu.

Mama was very surprised to see Pingu and Fuzz walk into the garden.

"Mama!" cried Pingu.

"A mammoth!" said Mama. "Where did you find him?"

"Down the lane," said Pingu.

"Come inside, Fuzz, and have some toast!"

"Fuzz," asked Mama. "Are you a real mammoth?"

Fuzz nodded, "Yes, I'm sure, I think."

It was not long before Pingu's neighbours had heard all about Fuzz. They raced over to his igloo to see what the fuss was about.

"A real Woolly Mammoth!" they cried as their cameras clicked. "Our town will be famous! Pingu will be famous!" they cried.

Soon, penguins and seals from all over the South Pole started to come and visit Fuzz. Fuzz was a very famous mammoth.

That was until one day...

Fuzz was sitting in the kitchen and yawned a big yawn. "I'm hot!" he

sighed, and he took off his woolly coat. "I had quite forgotten this was a woolly coat. It seemed just like a second skin!"

"Oh no!" cried Pingu. "You're not..."

"You're an elephant," said Mama. "Pingu!"

"Mama, I didn't know!" said Pingu.

"I'm sorry," said Fuzz. "I really had quite forgotten who I was but elephant sounds about right."

"It's coming back to me," sighed Fuzz. "It was a long, long time ago - I used to be a circus elephant . One day the circus just packed up and left me. I cried for weeks..."

"You poor thing," Mama patted him on the back. "Pingu you must let everyone know that Fuzz is not a mammoth."

"Can't you tell them, Mama? Please!" Pingu pleaded.

"No," said Mama. "It was your mistake, now go."

Pingu crept outside and stood on a barrel, "Hello, everyone!" he yelled.

"Where's the Mammoth?" the crowds yelled back.

"Well, um, Fuzz is not really a mammoth, he's an elephant!" Pingu replied sadly.

"An ELEPHANT!" cried the crowds angrily. "AN ELEPHANT!"

Pingu looked worried, but then the angry faces suddenly cracked up into smiles. Everyone was laughing, they thought it was a big joke.

"But I didn't mean for it to be a joke!" shouted Pingu. But the crowd didn't hear him because they were laughing so loud.

Pingu walked back inside, "I'm sorry, Mama."

"It was just a misunderstanding," smiled Mama. "We've got to get Fuzz home."

Pingu watched as six mighty albatrosses lifted Fuzz into the air and flew away. They were taking him to rejoin his circus.

"Bye, bye Fuzz!" he called. "It was great meeting you!"

"Bye, bye Pingu," Fuzz lifted his trunk to wave, "I'll try not to forget you - but you know what my memory's like!"

Pingu smiled to himself as he waved his new friend goodbye.

Pingu-drew-it-saurus

Pingu's made up some dinosaurs for you - can you match the names of the dinosaurs to the right dinosaur? There is one real dinosaur, do you know which one that is?

Answers on page 61.

Tyrannosaurus Rex
Spotasaurus

Sealasaurus
Iglooasaurus

Pinguasaurus

Ski Mix Up!

Pingu's been at it again. He was playing in the ski shed and has mixed up all the skis. Follow the squiggly lines to match the skis to the right penguin. Which is the spare pair of skis?

Turn to page 61 for the answers.

A Chilly Crossword

WAAK! Pingu's made up a crossword for you - read the clues carefully, then fill in the missing words and letters.

Down

1. What kind of bird is Pingu?
2. Robby is a _ _ _ _
3. Pingu lives in the South _ _ _ _

Across

1. Pingu's girlfriend's name is _ _ _ _ _
2. What's white and falls from the sky?
3. Pingu and his family live in an _ _ _ _ _
4. Pingu rides on one.

See page 61 for the answers.

Down 1. P i n g i
Across 2. S N O W F L A K E
Down 1 (cont.): P e n g u i n
Across 2 (right): S E a L
Down 3 / Across 3: I g L o O
Down 3 (cont.): N ... L
Across 4. S L E D g e

41

Sno'Business, Like Sno'Business

1. BANG! CLANK! BANG! Pingu and his friends were playing in their band. Robby banged the drums, Pingi played the guitar, Pinga rattled the tambourine and Pingu sung the songs. Their band was called the 'Frost Bites' and tonight was the night of their very first concert.

2. Tonight they were going to play in front of their first proper audience. The only audience they had played to before was Mama and Papa - and they'd worn earmuffs!

3. "Is everyone ready?" asked Pingu. "Make sure you have everything you need." Robby, Pinga and Pingi checked around them. "We're ready!" they cried.

4. "Look at all those penguins!" said Robby. "I'm nervous! I think I'll..."
"Don't worry," said Pingu. "Just start playing and you'll forget the audience. Come on, we're on!"

5. Pingu and his friends climbed up onto the stage and picked up their instruments. "Hello," Pingu yelled to the audience. "We are the Frost Bites!"
The Frost Bites started to play!

6. It was not long before they had played all their songs and their flippers were tired. "Good night!" called Pingu. But the audience wanted to hear another song. They clapped and cheered until Pingu and his friends came back on stage. They played three more songs and the audience kept clapping and cheering.

7. "That was great fun," yawned Pinga. "I think the audience liked us." "I think the audience loved us!" laughed Pingu. They had all enjoyed their very first concert.

8. It was not long before the Frost Bites became famous. They saw their pictures on the covers of magazines and they even appeared on television. "Oh," sighed Pingu. "I've always wanted to be famous!"

9. But being famous was very hard work. The Frost Bites still had to go to school and do their homework AND play in the band. They played a concert nearly every night!

10. But life isn't easy at the top! "Mama!" croaked Pingu pointing to his throat. "You've lost your voice," said Mama. "Now go to bed. You won't be able to sing." Pingu shook his head sadly.

11. A few days later, Robby came running over to see poor Pingu. "Look!" he cried holding up a magazine cover. "We've been forgotten! A new band, called the Steely Seals, have taken our place."

12. Pingu shrugged and two tears rolled down his cheeks. "It's all my fault!" he croaked sadly. "Don't worry Pingu," said Robby. "It was fun - it's time we did something else."

13. "Well," said Pingi. "The audience may have forgotten all about us. But at least we've got each other." The four friends nodded. "I wonder what we can do now," Pinga said thoughtfully.

14. "I know!" said Pingu jumping out of bed. "Why don't we become cowpenguins! We could call ourselves the, um, The Ranch Cubes!" The rest of the Frost Bites shook their heads, "NO!"

Shoebox Stars

Pingu and his friends were a little sad when their rock 'n' roll career was over. But Pingu had an idea to help them all remember their good times. A shoebox stage! It's easy to make!

You will need:

A shoebox
Coloured paper
Paints/Crayons/Felt tip pens
Safe glue
Round-ended scissors
Cardboard
Glitter and shiny paper
4 straws

How to make your Shoebox Theatre

1. First decide which side of the shoebox you want as the stage and then turn it on its side. The stage is the side touching the floor.

2. Paint a background onto the back of the theatre.

3. Cut out two pieces of paper or card in the shape of a curtain, paint them red and then stick it to the side of the shoebox, like Pingu has done. Decorate your stage, using your glitter and cutting out shapes.

5. Cut out Pingu and his friends on the opposite page, stick them onto cardboard then glue a straw to their backs - this will help you move them about on stage.

4. Use your scissors to cut a slit - this is where your band can come on and off the stage.

Party Spot!

WAAK! Pingu has been naughty again! Look at these two pictures carefully, there are seven differences between them, can you find them all?

Turn to page 61 for the answers.

1,2,3, POP!

This is a great game for two players. First you have to choose a number from 1 to 6 - you can't both have the same number! Now take it in turn to throw the die - each time you throw your number write your name on a balloon. When all the balloons have been popped, see how many balloons you've popped. The player who's popped the most balloons is the winner.

"I'd rather be playing or eating," Pingu moaned as he tidied up his room.
"Oooh, look at this." Pingu lifted Pinga's ballet tutu from a pile of clothes on
the floor.

"What a silly looking thing," he said to himself. "I wonder... umm." He put
the tutu on and walked over to the mirror.

He twirled, just like he had seen Pinga twirl. "Well..." he
said to himself.

"PINGU!" cried Robby.

Pingu turned around, "What are you doing here?"

"Your Mama told me where
you were," smiled Robby. "Pingu
what are wearing?"

Pingu had quite forgotten he was
wearing the tutu.

Robby suddenly burst out
laughing, "Wait until I tell
everybody!" Robby ran out of the
room and out of the
igloo. "Pingu wants to

be a ballet dancer! Ha! HA!"

Pingu did one final twirl, "Well," he thought to himself. "I make a good ballet dancer."

Pingu went to find Pinga who was playing in the back garden. "Pinga," called Pingu. "When is your next ballet lesson?"

"This afternoon," Pinga replied. "Why do you want to know?"

"I want to be a ballet dancer!" said Pingu.

"You! Ha! Ha!" laughed Pinga.

"Pinga, I really want to be a ballet dancer," said Pingu.

"It's good fun, we can go together. Let's get ready," said Pinga.

She helped Pingu get dressed in a leotard and then helped tie up his ballet shoes.

"You look the part!" she smiled. "Come on, let's go!"

They waddled along to the ballet school - Madam Plinski had already started the class.

"Sorry, we're late," said Pinga. "My
brother's joining our class today."
Pingu bowed to Madam Plinski.
"Welcome," she said.
Pingu was the only boy penguin in the class.

   He tripped over his own flippers and flopped instead of flipped. "Oh dear!"
he sighed. "I've got two left flippers. Ballet dancing isn't as easy as I thought
it would be! I think I'll take up ice hockey."
"You could join my ice hockey team," suggested Pinga. "Let's go, our ballet
class has finished."

   Pingu found his friends waiting for him outside the ballet school.
His friends were laughing and pointing.
"I'm going home," said Pingu. "And Robby, I'm going to pick up my
mechanical fish from your place on
my way home."
Pingu stamped off, while his friends
kept laughing.

Mama's Bedtime Story

Mama tucked Pingu and Pinga into bed, then she went to turn out the light.
SQU-EAK!
"Mama," cried Pingu. "What was that?"

"It was just a little squeak," whispered Mama. "It's nothing to be afraid of."
"How do you know?" asked Pingu.
"Well, I'll tell you how I know..." and Mama started her little story.

Fluff liked living under the bed, she had lived under one all her life. At first she had lived with her family, then one day it was time to get her very own bed.

She loved her bed. It was dark and dusty and there was enough dust to make lots of fluff balls. Making fluff balls kept her very busy. Fluff worked very hard during the day and slept soundly at night.

That was until one night... Fluff was tucked up inside her little bed. She dreamed that she was making the biggest fluff ball in the whole world.
"ARRRRGGGH!"

Fluff jumped out of bed. "What was that?" she cried. She crept out from under her bed to find out what was happening.

A little penguin was sitting straight up in his bed, her mother came into the room. "What's the matter?" she whispered.

"I heard a squeaky-snoring sound," the little penguin cried. "It was really scary."

"Don't worry," said the little penguin's mother. "There is nothing here to scare you. Go back to sleep."

"The poor little penguin," sighed Fluff. "I didn't hear a thing. I heard nothing at all."

Fluff crept back to bed and went to sleep.

"MAMA!" The little penguin woke up again. Her mother came back and sat with her daughter until she fell asleep again.

Fluff was very worried, "I wonder what the little penguin is so afraid of," she thought to herself before she nodded back to sleep.

Fluff woke with a start - peeking out over the bed clothes, she saw two big eyes staring at her.

"What do you want?" she cried with fright.

"I sleep on top of the bed," whispered the little penguin. "And you've been scaring me."

"I couldn't scare a fly!" said Fluff. "I wouldn't scare a fly!"

"Well, you scared a penguin," smiled the little penguin.

"But how could I?" asked Fluff. "I'm so small and you're so tall!"

"You were snoring and whistling," laughed the little penguin. "I thought you were a... well, I didn't know that a little bug could make such a big noise."

Fluff smiled to herself, "So that's what scared you, my snoring. Ha! Ha! But I am so very sorry."

"Good night," said the little penguin. "Sleep tight. I know I will, now that I know that there is nothing to be afraid of!"

"Sweet dreams," called Fluff.

"But, Mama," said Pingu. "How do you know it's true?"

"Because that little penguin was me," smiled

Shadow Play

Look! Pingu and Pinga are making shadow. Can you guess what they are? Look closely.

1.

2.

3.

4.

5.

6.

DOOG GNITH

Now see if you can unscramble Pingu's words to find out what he is saying to you.

Answers on Page 61.

Answers

Page 11 Post Sort

A. comes from Australia

B. comes from Holland

C. comes from Wales

D. comes from Scotland.

Page 25 Going Dotty

Pingu drew a clown seal on a unicycle.

Page 31 Work it Out!

Pingu is going to wash the dishes and Nut is going to do the dusting.

Page 39 Pingu-drew-it-saurus

A	=	Pingusaurus
B	=	Sealasaurus
C	=	Tyrannosaurus Rex
D	=	Iglooasaurus
E	=	Spotasaurus

C is the odd one out because all the other dinosaurs have been made up by Pingu.

Page 40 Ski Mix Up!

Pair D is the spare pair of skis - A belong to Pingu, B belong to Pingi, C belong to Ping and E belong to Pinga.

Page 41 A Chilly Crossword

Across:
1. Pingi
2. Snowflake
3. Igloo
4. Sledge.

Down:
1. Penguin
2. Seal
3. Pole.

Page 48 Party Spot!

Page 60 Shadow Play

1 = Seal		4 = Pig	
2 = Rabbit		5 = Penguin	
3 = Dog		6 = Bird	

Pingu is saying "GOOD NIGHT"